Is there a shindig, a social soirée,
a big-bash, a party for your special day?
Will there be streamers, family and fun?
Perhaps I could go. Would you like me to come?

Santa loves birthdays with all their tradition.
I know he would give me exclusive permission—
to come to your wing-ding, your hullabaloo.
He probably wishes that he could come, too.

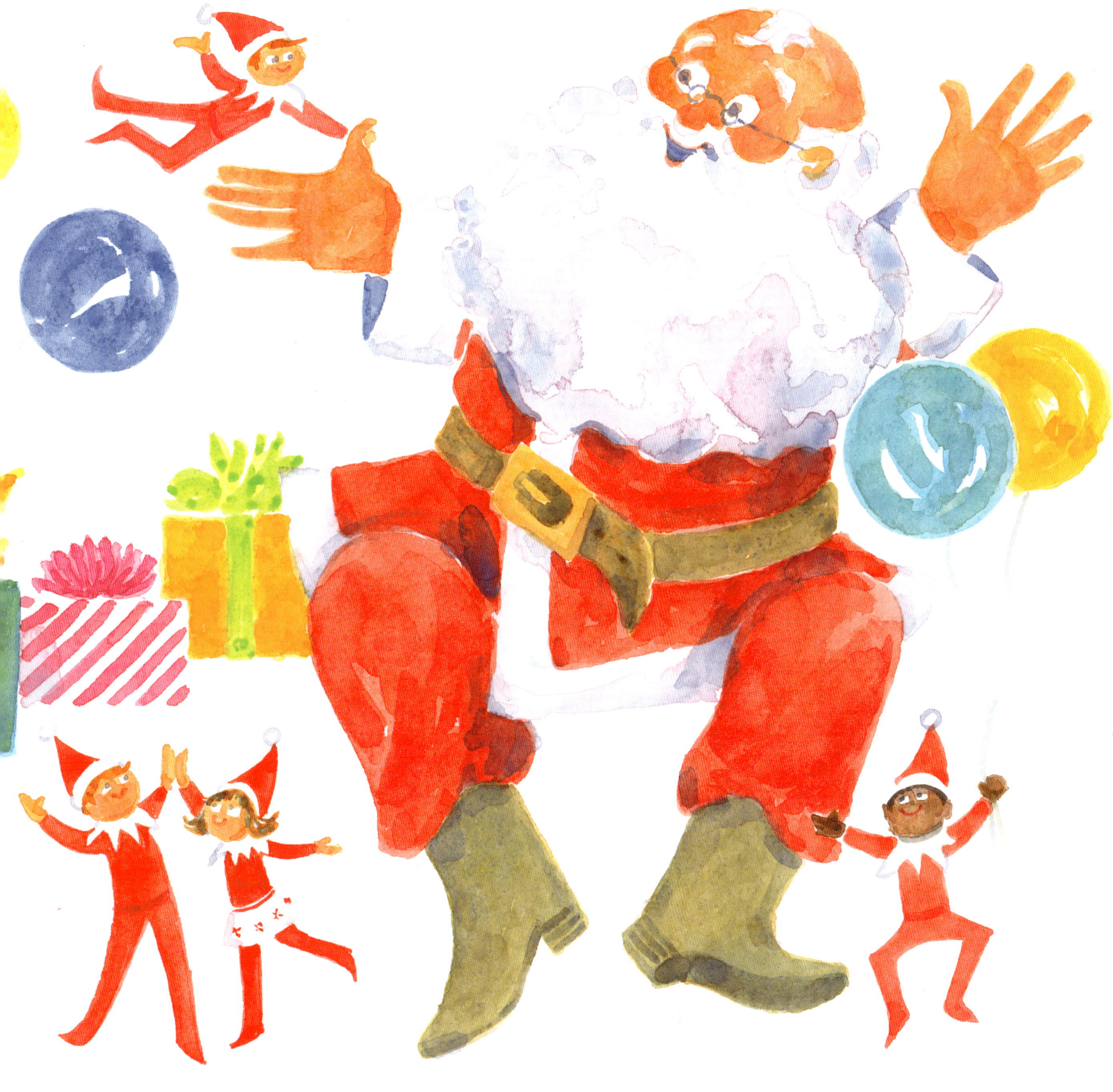

Please come

First, you should make me an elf invitation
then lay out my clothes for your big celebration.
Santa will nod and give me a grin
because he'll be sure you want me to attend.

I'll see his eyes gleam
with a hint of a twinkle.
He'll stretch out his palm
and elf dust will sprinkle.
Like Christmas magic,
it floats through the air.
"This dust is for birthdays,"
he'll whisper with care.

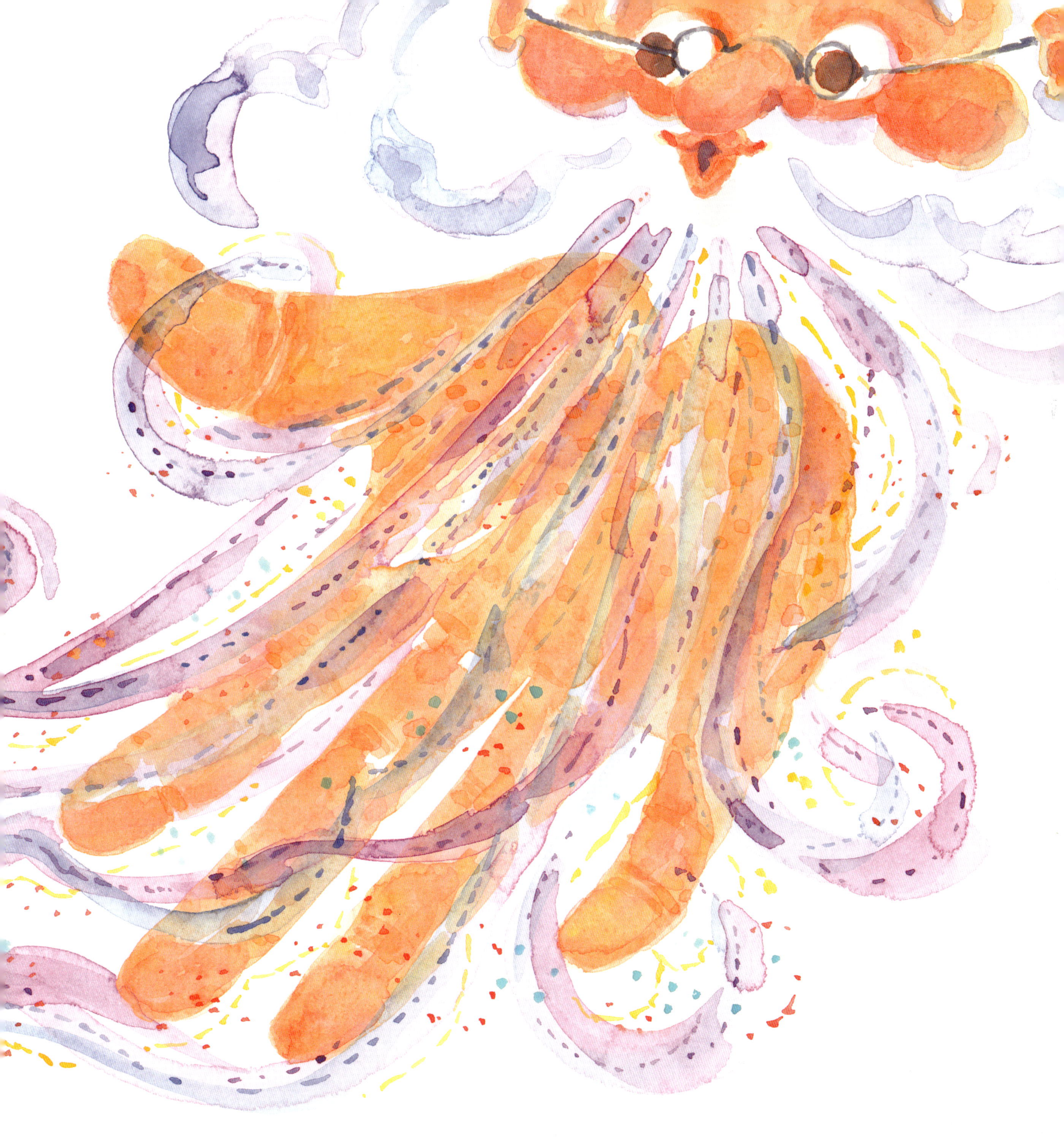

He'll tell me to hurry and join in the fun
for twenty-four hours since work must be done.
I'll leap up to thank him then bolt through the door.
In less than a minute, I'll magically soar.

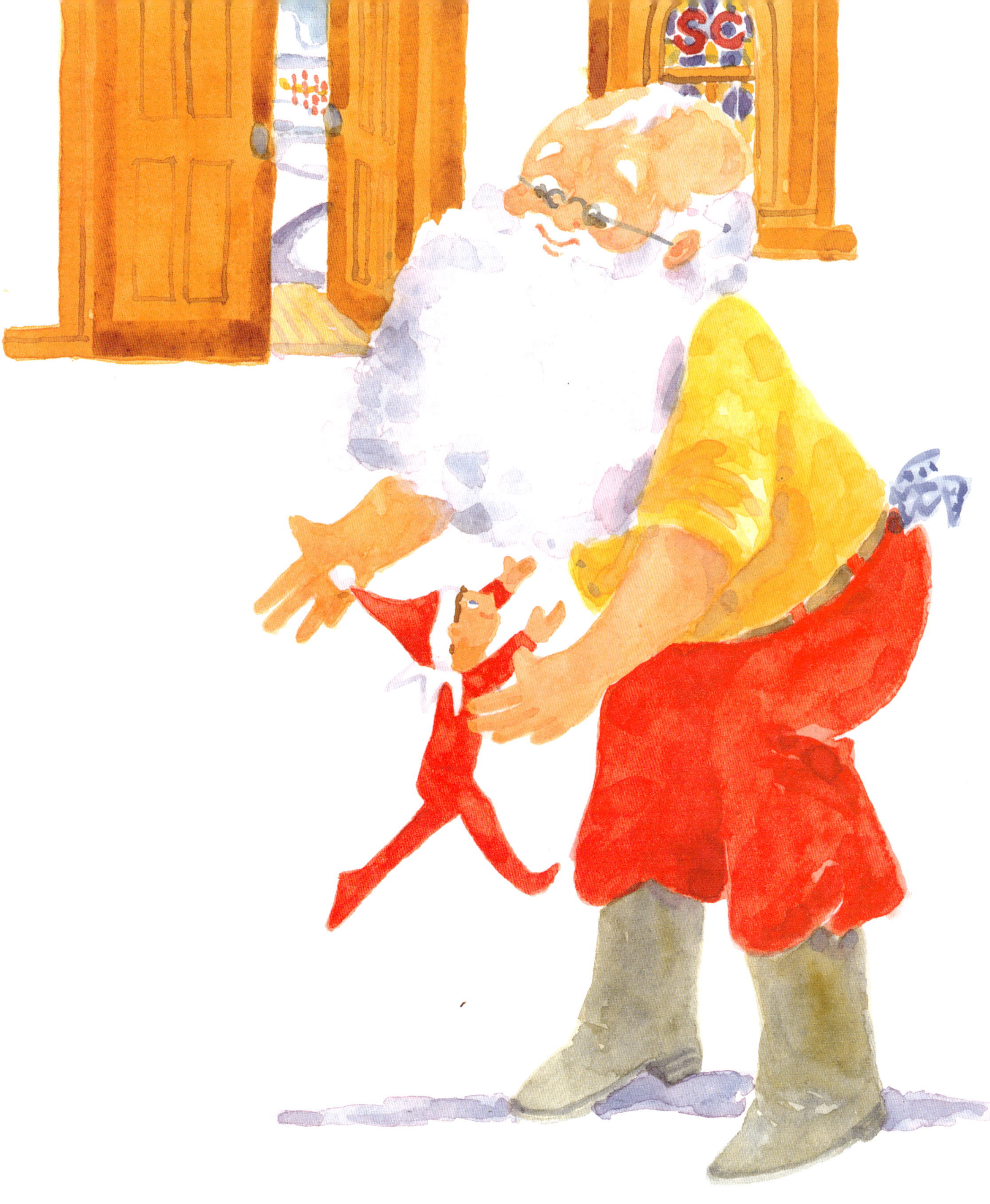
SC

With a swiftness reserved
for elves half my age,
I'll be back at your home as
you take center stage.
Together we'll honor a year
that has passed,
and make some
new memories,
ones that will last.

...RTHDAY

THE MAIN MAN!

Happy Birthday!

I won't have a token, a present, or prize
since that could be tough given my tiny size.
But I have an idea I'd like to propose—
a North Pole tradition and here's how it goes:

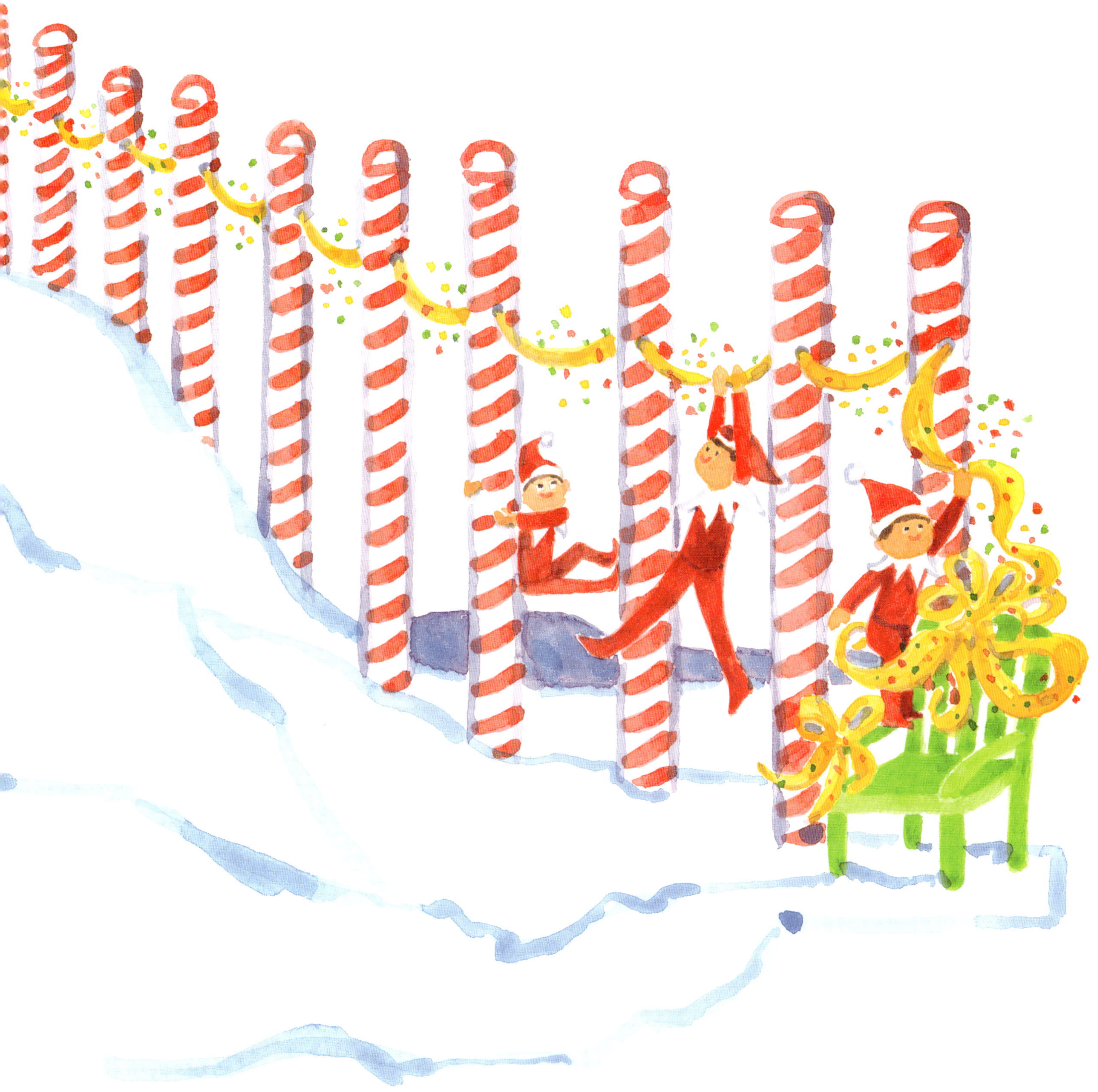

I'll spring into action
and pick out a chair
to trim like a tree with
my own special flair.
I'll decorate with treasures
and fabulous finds
and make use of trinkets
of all different kinds.

BIRTHDAY POP CORN

Perhaps I'll be sensible, careful and wise
to choose things you need for my special surprise.
I could also be silly and go for a laugh,
by making a scene with your fuzzy giraffe.

I might be crafty with
ribbons and bows
or use crayons and pencils
on signs I compose.
How 'bout balloons filled
with candy to eat?
First you must pop them;
then get your treat.

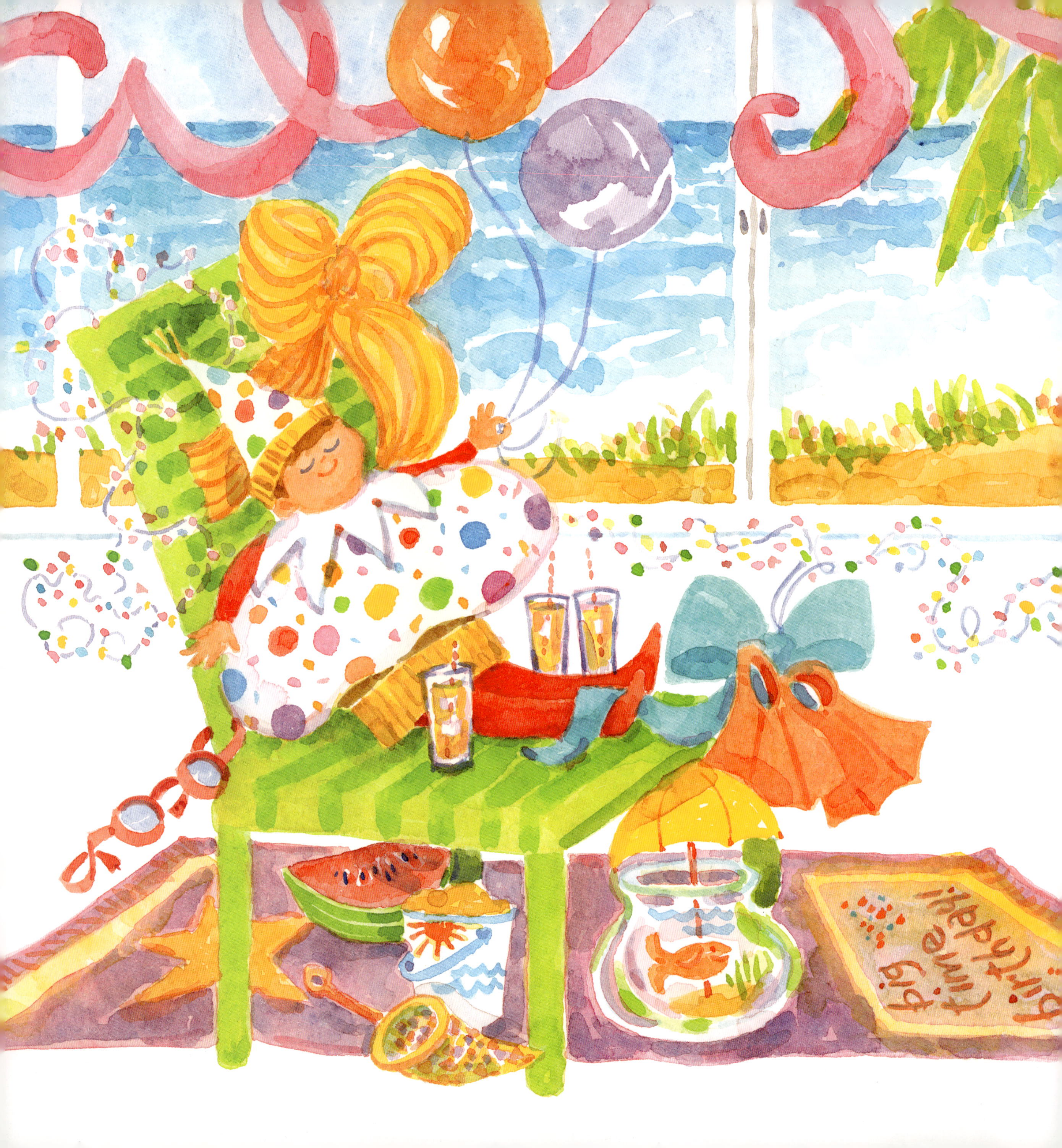

With a last dash of whimsy thrown in for good measure,
your chair is now ready for your birthday pleasure.
Before our eyes meet and I make my debut,
there's one final thing that I really must do.
I'll dress in my costume and hide in a place
where I can first spy the big smile on your face.
Our game will begin when you dash out of bed.
You'll see what I've done while you rested your head.

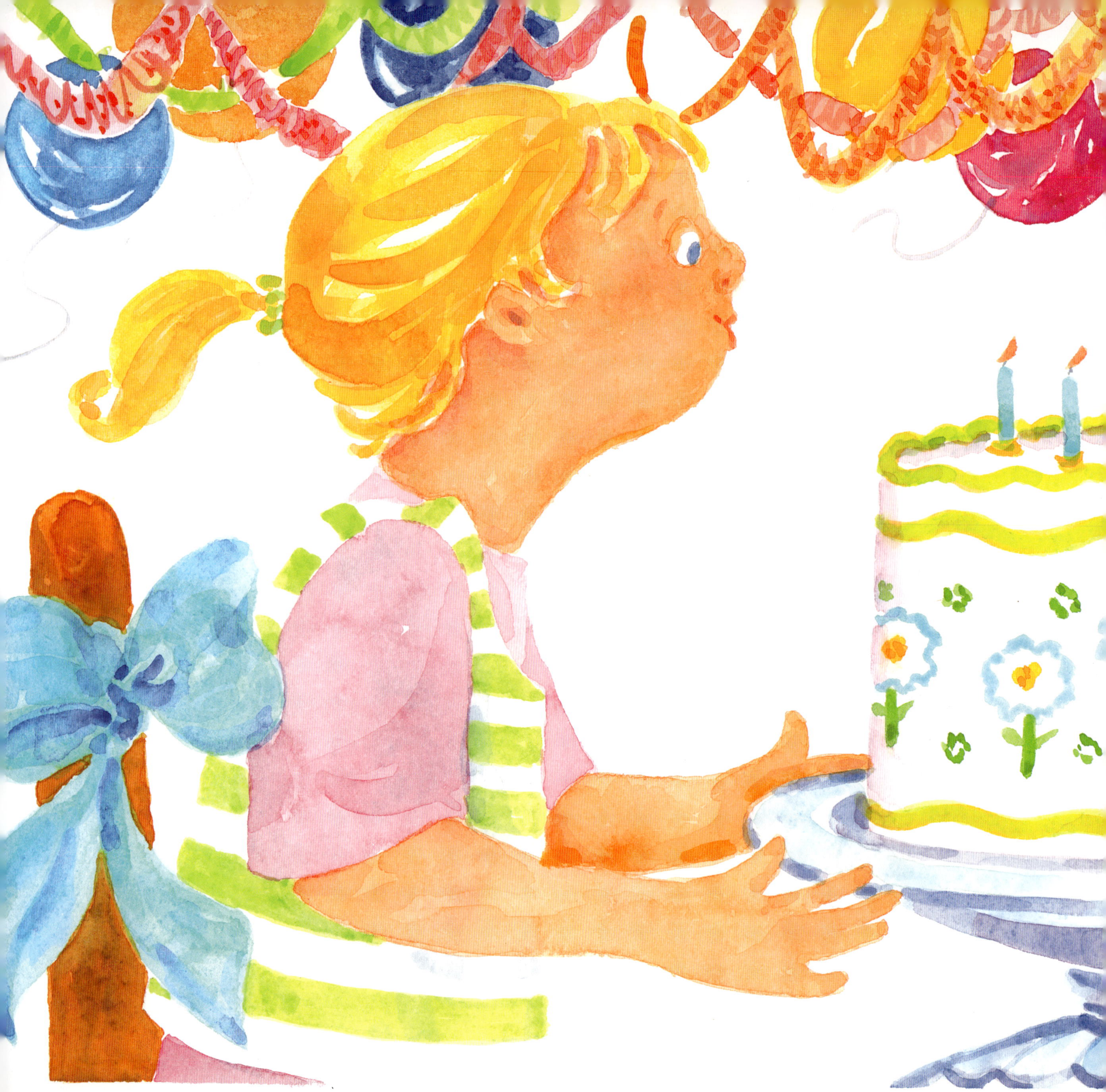

Your big day's just starting
there's much more in store:
like presents, and singing,
and wishes galore.
Your cake will have candles
all glowing, no doubt.
We'll hear a big "whoosh"
as you blow them all out.

While you celebrate I'll be beaming with pride,
from a shelf or a frame or wherever I hide.
Finally, our day will come to an end.
I'll fly back to Santa and with my elf friends—

We'll cheer and we'll shout, "Hip-Hip-Hooray,"
and we will all wish you a Happy Birthday!

® and © 2013 by CCA and B, LLC®

All rights reserved. No part of this publication may be reproduced, stored in a retrieval system, or transmitted, in any form or by any means, electronic, mechanical, photocopying, recording, or otherwise, without express prior written permission of the authors.

ISBN: 978-0-9843651-9-7

www.elfontheshelf.com

1174 Hayes Industrial Drive
Marietta, GA 30062
www.ccaandb.com

Elf Invitation

Dear __Elf__,

Can you come to my Birthday P[arty]
yes/no? ✓ Elf. Love
from [name] and family [signature]
xoxo